S

**This book is to be returned on or before
the last date stamped below.**

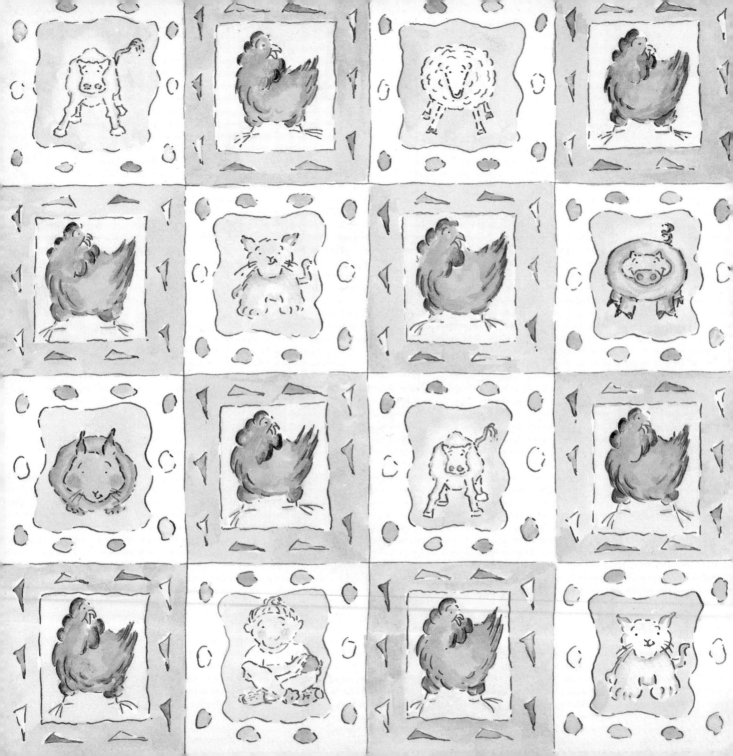

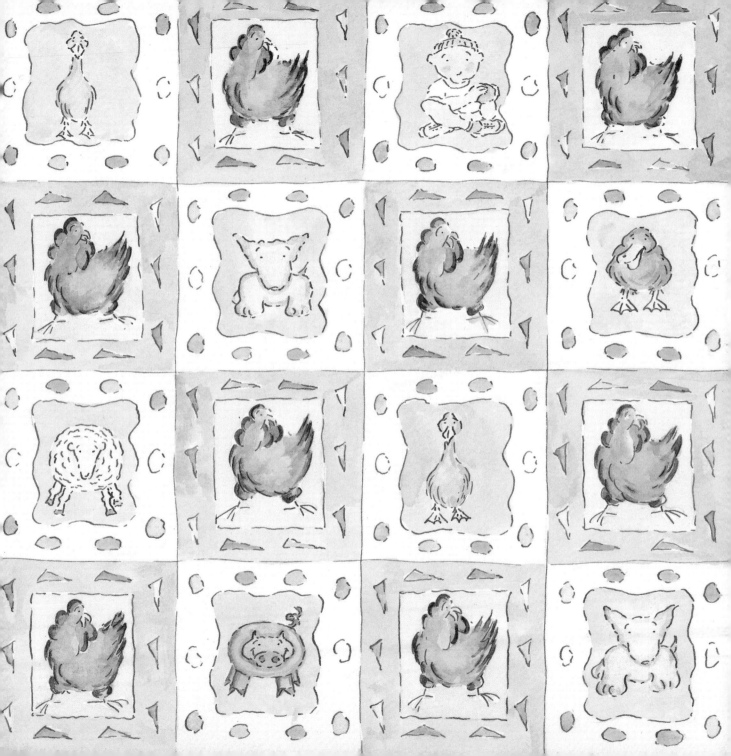

For Fiona

First published in Great Britain 1987 by Orchard Books
Published in Picture Lions 1989

Picture Lions is an imprint of the Children's Division,
part of the Collins Publishing Group
8 Grafton Street, London W1X 3LA

Text and illustrations copyright © 1987 by Siobhan Dodds

Printed by Warners of Bourne and London

Conditions of Sale: This book is sold subject to the condition that
it shall not, by way of trade or otherwise, be lent, re-sold, hired out
or otherwise circulated without the publisher's prior consent in
any form of binding or cover other than that in which it is
published and without a similar condition including this condition
being imposed on the subsequent purchaser.

Elizabeth Hen

Siobhan Dodds

COLLINS
PICTURE LIONS
in association with
ORCHARD BOOKS

One day Elizabeth Hen laid an egg.

Next she told the farmer's wife
with her five children,

the cat with her six kittens,

the pig with her seven piglets,

then the dog
with her eight puppies,

and the duck
with her nine ducklings.

and then the goose
with her four goslings.

Feeling very proud,
she went to tell her friends.
First she told the cow
with her two calves,

then the sheep
with her three lambs,

Last of all she told the rabbit
with her ten babies.

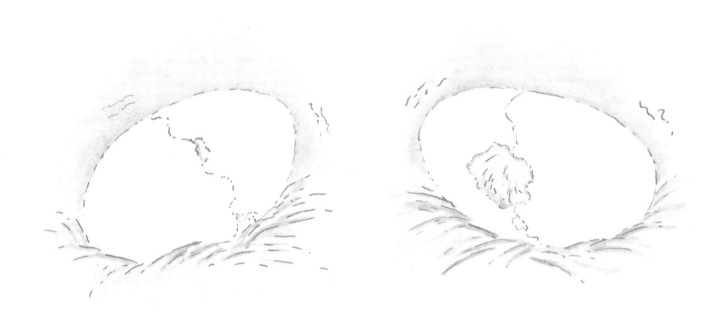

But when Elizabeth Hen
returned to her egg,
something strange was happening.

The egg was cracked
and rocking from side to side.
TAP-TAP-TAP! went the egg,
and out popped a chick.

Elizabeth Hen was as proud as could be.

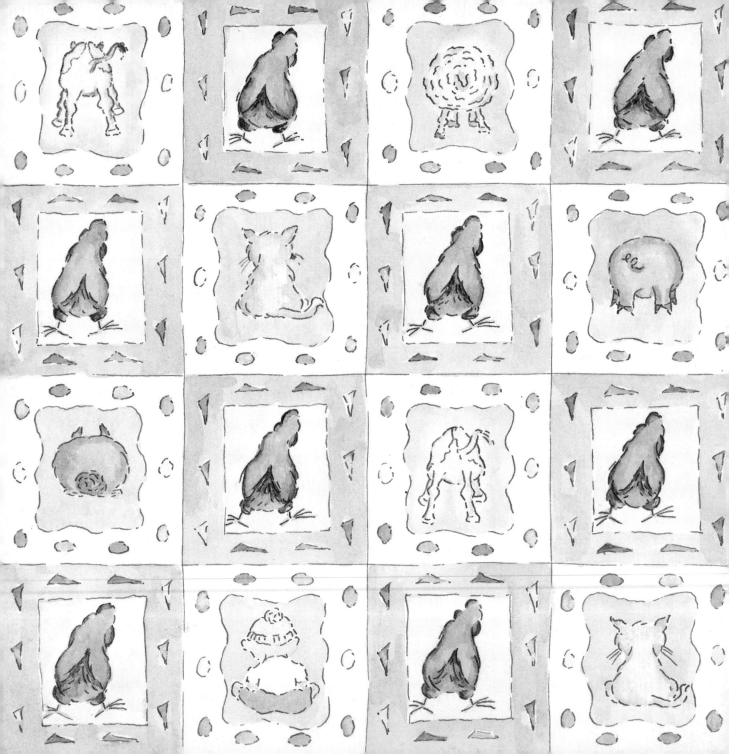

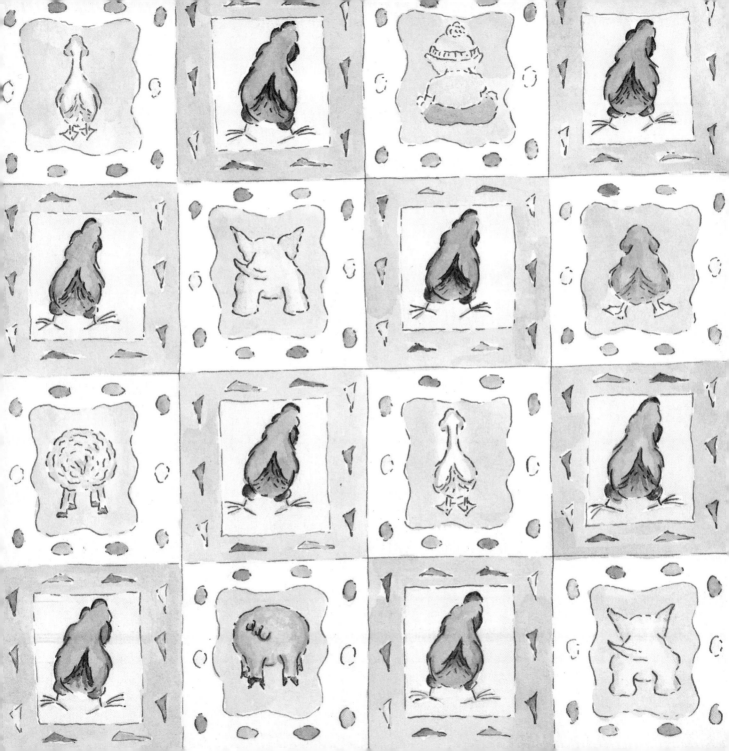